LUPE

FIVE BROTHERS

BOOK 4.5

MELISSA BELL

FIVE BROTHER SERIES

BOOK #4.5

By

Melissa Bell

ACKNOWLEDGMENTS

Michele Thompson
Editing/Proofreading

Editing
J.J. Jarret

CHAPTER 1

Lupe's mother worked two jobs to make ends meet. He always felt guilty when he came home from the library to find his mother heading out the door at 9:00 pm to start her night shift at the hotel. At fourteen, he'd already been pretty sure of who he wanted to be and who he was as a person. He wanted to be a doctor; he knew if he could get the grades, one day he'd be able to take care of his mother and pay her back for all her hard work. She kept a roof over their heads, food on the table, and the power and heat had never been cut off, even on his mother's minimum wage.

Lupe had come home at the end of his third year in college as a med student to find his mother sleeping peacefully. He walked over to the couch and leaned down to kiss her on the forehead and found her cold to the touch. He sat down on the floor beside her and lifted her hand to his cheek; he felt as though he'd failed her in more ways than one. Every time she called him, she would ask if he'd met anyone nice. He would always respond that he didn't have time for dating, and then he'd change the subject. He knew his mother wanted grandchildren, but between the university and the fact nobody drew his attention away from his studies, he hadn't even considered dating. Sure the girls would all flirt with him. He was a good-looking guy, it all came down to timing, and he had a plan. He glanced at his mother, not sure what to do. After all, it was just the two of them.

His grandparents had disowned his mother long before they passed away. They wouldn't even look at her after telling them she was pregnant with him. Apparently, she had disgraced their name within the community.

Lupe's father paid for his education, but it still wasn't enough to cover living on campus and the cost of his books. He'd buried his mother alone in the pouring rain, using the last of her savings. When Houston knocked on his front door, Lupe was about to surrender the lease on the rental house he'd grown up in. His mother must have been watching over him from above. Houston explained their connection and gave him a sales pitch he couldn't pass up. He spent the night packing, and they headed to Lafayette the following day.

~

Mount Cotton, Queensland, Australia

Lupe woke abruptly to the sound of his brother knocking on his door. He quickly shoved his legs into a pair of sweatpants and pulled on a t-shirt. "Incoming!"

He jogged along the hall to the garage door as the lights of an approaching vehicle burned his eyes. When he entered the infirmary, Brody was busy turning on the lights and collecting a trolley full of sterilized packets of gauze and instruments. "I'm not a fucking vet. If I have to say it one more time I'm gonna start shaving your fur off. Shift goddamn it, now." he said, taking on his doctor's voice. "Fuck my life! I'm not in the mood for this, I've just done a double shift at the hospital and I have to be back there in about four hours. Brody you're on babysitting duty once this is done." he grumbled. He took a calming breath and then went to work on extracting the bullet and stitching up the wound. He stepped back from his brother with a tired sigh and removed his surgical gloves. "And the crowd goes wild. Hoorahhhhh." he took a bow, "Thank you, thank you and good night, next time, try not to get shot! I'm outta here,"

Lupe dragged his feet back in the direction of his room, jumped into a quick shower, and washed off. Although he was tired, the water running over his honed abs was enough to harden his shaft. Lupe soaped up his hand and turned his body to the tiles placing one palm flat on the surface while his other circled his girth. He squeezed the base, then ran it firmly to the crown of his circumcised tip. He bit his lower lip to prevent making any noise. As he closed his eyes, he angled the front of his body away from the spray of the water. He imagined what it would be like to have warm slippery wet skin against his chest as his body cages his mate's back. His cock slid along the creviced curve of their ass as they tilted their head to the side to give him access to their shoulder, his canines throbbed in rhythm with his blood rushing through his pulsating member as his impending orgasm grew closer. He fucked his palm harder, his hip undulating with the need to spend his seed. As he tasted blood on his lip, he imagined his bite puncturing his mate's skin as he claimed them. His climax weakened his already tired knees, and he rested his forehead against the tiles to catch his breath on a sob.

He rinsed the solitude and loneliness from his body with a resolved sigh, then turned off the shower. He briskly dried himself and then headed back to bed after double-checking that his alarm was set. He closed his eyes and threw his arm around the pillow beside him, sinking into an all too brief amount of sleep.

The sound of his alarm split through the air, waking him up abruptly. He dragged himself out of bed after what only felt like a ten-minute snooze. He'd fallen into the same pattern of existence over the previous month – get up, get dressed, report for duty at the local hospital, spend the day in an emergency room with all manner of dramas and complications.

This morning had begun with an in-flamed appendix which he'd referred to the surgical team. A workplace accident, once stabilized, the patient was then moved to the burns unit. He called for a psych evaluation for a teenager who had unsuccessfully at-tempted suicide. Although he was pretty sure the patient wouldn't try overdosing on pills again. However, he wasn't convinced that it would be a one-off attempt. By lunchtime, he'd lost count of the cases he'd seen, and as quick as the emergency waiting room emptied, it refilled. If it wasn't from walk-ins, it was via the ambulance services.

At the end of his lunch break, he raced to the on-site pharmacy to grab a couple of pre-natal kits for his brother's mates, who he believed to be pregnant. He yawned as he stuffed them into his locker and then returned to finish his shift. His wolf's senses made his nose so sensitive that he could identify a subtle change in a woman's hormones, giving her perspiration a slightly sweet scent when pregnant.

Tate and Jasmine had moved into their new home above the dance studio. Lupe parked at the back of the premises.

He'd decided to call in on the way home to present them with a housewarming gift. He knocked on the door and waited. He was tired after his shift, but he'd taken the time to pick up prenatal vitamins and a home pregnancy kit from the hospital. He'd also grabbed a large bunch of flowers from the hospital's florist in a decorative vase.

The door opened, and he caught the most intoxicating scent. His heart raced, his pupils dilated, and his cock stiffened. "Here, let me help you with that," He heard the dark timber of a man's voice make the offer. Their eyes met as their hands brushed, his nostrils flared, and a shiver of recognition ran down his spine. The word 'Mine' growled loud and clear in his mind.

CHAPTER 2

Lupe had only planned on a drop-and-run visit. However, the circumstances had greatly changed. He'd been blindsided by his own body's manic release of chemicals inside his brain after scenting his mate. Not trusting it, he cleared his throat, then answered, "Thanks."

'Fuck! What the hell's with my voice?' He wondered.

"I'm Henry, and you are?" the tall, handsome man that stood to match his impressive six feet, three inches asked.

"Lupe, Lupe Garcia. I'm Tate's brother."

A smile spread over Henry's face, "Nice to meet you, Lupe. The others are inside." he continued to hold the door open for Lupe to enter. He didn't miss the sudden intake of breath and the dilation of Henry's brown eyes to black as he did so. Lupe's heart sped up as he walked from the entry to the main living area. He stopped mid-stride unexpectedly, and Henry's momentum aligned him at Lupe's back with a slight bump. Lupe's hand reached out to the wall beside him to steady himself. "Sorry, I can't remember if I locked my car. I hadn't planned to come in." with a little bit of ducking and weaving, they changed positions, and Lupe opened the door, and with his key in his hand, he engaged the automatic central locking system. The lights flashed, and there was a little beep, beep to indicate the vehicle was secure.

He turned back around after closing the door, expecting to find the entryway empty. Instead, he found Henry standing there waiting for him in what looked to be a trance. Lupe realized his mate's focus had gone from his ass to the bulge behind the fly of his zipper, making it even more obvious that Lupe was turned on, revved up, and raring to go. He shifted the brown paper bag in his hand to hide his excitement at finding his mate. A scream broke the silence, and Henry spun on his heel, with Lupe moving quickly behind him. The Senator was on the floor clutching at his chest, "Lupe, do something." Tate ordered, putting his arm around Jasmine to stop her from getting in the way. Lupe pushed past Henry, dropping the brown paper bag on the couch as he looked at the unconscious Senator's paling face. He shoved the coffee table out of the way and began to perform CPR. "Call a bus, tell them it's a cardiac arrest." he continued the chest compressions. "Henry, go and meet the ambulance."

Even after the ambulance arrived, he refused to stop until they had the defibrillator charged and ready to go. He followed them out to the ambulance holding the mask over the Senator's mouth and nose, squeezing the respiratory bag to keep the air flowing through his lungs and, therefore, his brain.

Henry stood back and watched on in shock. His boss was fine just half an hour ago, "Which hospital?" he called to Lupe.

"Bayside General," he yelled back as the ambulance driver closed the doors and then raced to climb into the driver's seat. Flicking on the lights and sirens, Henry dug in his pocket for the keys to the Senator's vehicle. Taking a deep breath, he slid behind the wheel and started the engine, and threw it into drive, following behind the ambulance as close as possible. His palm slammed into the steering wheel, and he cursed at not even giving the Senator's daughter a thought; but when he saw lights fly around the corner and fall in behind to dog his tail, he knew Tate had things under control with Jasmine.

When the ambulance's back doors were finally opened at the hospital's emergency entrance, Lupe jumped from inside to shadow the Senator through to a cubicle. He became Doctor Lupe Garcia and commanded the small area with precision. Inserting a breathing tube, instructing the nurse to set up an IV with fluids and blood thinners, and within seconds of arriving, the Senator was hooked to a heart monitor and was intubated. He then called for a consult from the hospital's cardiology department. Sadly, while they waited for the specialist to respond to his request, the Senator's monitoring system alarms rang out as he crashed.

Lupe hadn't lost a patient, and he prayed that his sister-in-law's father wouldn't be his first. He used the defibrillator to try to kick start the Senator's heart.

Henry could see the determination on Lupe's face as he tried everything to resuscitate Senator Adam Winters.

Doctor Lucas James entered the cubicle in time to hear Lupe call out, "Clear!"

The Senator's body bucked from the jolt of power that surged through him. But the monitor was still showing a flat line.

Henry moved forward as Lupe prepared to inject epinephrine into the Senator's IV, his hand curled gently around Lupe's wrist.

"He's gone," he said barely above a whisper.

"No!" Lupe continued his attempts at bringing the Senator back, even though he knew Henry was right.

Dr. Lucas James observed the interaction between the two men. Then picked up the chart from the foot of the bed and pronounced the time of passing as he scribbled it on the file and signed it off.

"Dr. Garcia, a moment, please?" Dr. Lucas James insisted. Lupe was aware of who the man was. He had a well-known name in the cardiology department, and as Lupe's senior, he couldn't afford to blow him off.

"Yes sir," he stepped around Henry and followed to an area away from the prying eyes of the team now preparing the Senator for his daughter to say her final goodbyes.

Lucas said, "I like it when you call me that." he picked an invisible piece of lint off Lupe's shoulder with a sigh. "I'd like you to consider coming to work under me in my department."

Lupe frowned at the man's unbelievable tackiness, given that the Senator was now dead. "Um thanks for the offer but I prefer the E.R., if that's everything I need to let my sister-in-law know about her father."

"Of course," Dr. Lucas slid a card into the top pocket of Lupe's shirt. "Call me, I'm sure I can persuade you to change your mind over dinner."

Henry had been watching the way that Lupe's posture changed. His back had straightened defensively when the other man picked at something on his shoulder. He wasn't sure he understood why, but his feet moved before his mind registered it. He made it within earshot as the guy slipped something into Lupe's pocket and made a forward comment that Lupe felt uncomfortable with, and it agitated Henry.

Henry's fingers drifted to Lupe's pocket, where he found the card with the other doctor's name, phone number, and address on it. He flipped it over between his fingertips a couple of times, then returned it to Dr. Lucas James. His eye's bugged out when he looked at Henry, a tall man of around six feet, four inches and built like a finely honed machine, in a suit. He quickly cleared his throat and took a step back, "I have a patient..." his words died off as Henry glanced at Lupe.

"I think we should do this together, don't you? I'm not sure how Jasmine is going to take the news, I'd like you to be there just in case."

Lupe was speechless. He simply nodded at Dr. Lucas, then with Henry's hand in the small of his back, he turned and headed towards the waiting room to find his brother and the Senator's daughter.

CHAPTER 3

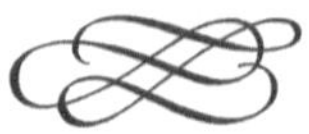

D r. Lucas watched as the two men walked away. He clenched his jaw several times as his mind ticked over concerning Dr. Garcia's blatant rejection of his advances. His eyes squinted at the possessive hand resting on Lupe's lower back, and he had to bite the inside of his cheek to stop himself from saying something aloud. Once they were clear of the doors to the waiting room, he approached the nearest nurse and asked for the paperwork to request an autopsy.

With the piece of paper in his hand, he returned to the Senators' cubicle and slid the document into the file requiring the family's signature to release the body.

Jasmine jumped up from her seat when she saw Lupe and Henry walk into the emergency waiting room. She wiped away the tears streaming down her face with the back of her hand, "Is he okay? Can I see him now?"

Henry stepped forward to wrap her in his arms, "I'm sorry sweetheart, Lupe did everything he could to save him but it was his time."

Tate grabbed his brother by the back of the head and pulled him into a bear hug, "You alright?" he whispered.

Lupe was so numb and in shock from losing his first patient, Jasmine's father, and he was unable to speak past the golf ball of emotion lodged in his throat. Finally, he pushed away from Tate and turned to Jasmine, who ran at him, throwing her arms around him. He only managed to choke out an, "I'm so sorry." before his voice cracked, and he was forced to pause.

A nurse seemed to appear from nowhere and offered to take Jasmine in to see her father for the last time before he was taken away. "There is some paperwork for you to sign, then you can stay with him for as long as you like." She escorted Jasmine and Tate through the swinging doors.

Henry reached out to Tate, "I'm going to take Lupe straight home. I don't think he's fit to drive in his present state. You okay with that?"

Tate looked briefly towards Lupe, then with a firm nod, he replied, "Take care of him for me, and don't hesitate to let me know if he needs anything."

"Will do."

Henry ushered Lupe out to where he'd parked the Senator's vehicle. He pressed the button to unlock the central locking mechanism, opened the passenger door for him, and then waited for Lupe to settle into the leather seat. He closed the door and rounded the front of the SUV to climb in behind the wheel.

They drove back to the Five Brothers headquarters. Henry couldn't help himself. He had to ask, "Did I interrupt anything between you and the good Doctor Lucas James?"

"No… absolutely not!" Lupe thought about it for a moment before elaborating further for the benefit of the man he was drawn to. "Never been there and have no plans on ever crossing that bridge with him. I'd prefer not to get tangled up in the hospital's spider web."

"Good, because I hate to say it, but the man comes across as quite a sadistic bastard. I… Fuck - I need a drink." he sighed heavily, running his palms over his suit-covered thighs.

"Me too! Come on." Lupe opened his door and climbed out. He dug in his pocket and found his keys to unlock the house's front door, leaving it open for Henry to follow. He headed straight for the kitchen cupboard to grab a couple of glasses. Meeting Henry's grief-stricken eyes, he led him to his room. He pulled a bottle of Glenfiddich down from the top of his closet. It had been a graduation gift from his brothers, but he'd never been inclined to open it until now. He broke the seal, uncorked the bottle, and then poured a heavy dose into both glasses.

Passing one to Henry, he lifted his in the air and made a toast, "To better days."

Henry raised his, "A-Fucking-Men!"

Lupe tossed his glass back and swallowed the contents in one belt, then said, "Make yourself at home, I need to wash the smell of the hospital off me. There's spare clothes in the dresser drawers help yourself, you can't drive anywhere now." he added as he walked into his private bathroom. "I won't be long. Can you pour me another?"

Henry swirled the amber remains in his glass, wishing he could put his finger on why he found himself so attracted to the much younger man. He heard the water turn on in the shower and gulped the last of his drink down. Sitting the empty glass beside Lupe's, he walked to where Lupe told him he would find something comfortable to change into. He kicked his shoes and socks off, followed by his tailored threads. Butt naked, he retrieved a pair of black sweatpants and pulled them on, then poured two more glasses. He paced towards the bathroom door, then turned around and paced back to the bed. Each time getting closer to where Lupe was and further away from the bed. Henry went on his instincts that at the moment were telling him that the younger man on the other side of the door needed him. He rested his hand flat against the timber, then his forehead as he tried to reason with himself. His heart raced as he finally admitted to himself that he, too, needed comfort.

His neatly manicured nails scraped the paint gently as his fingers curled into a fist, and he softly wrapped his knuckles on it, then waited for Lupe to answer. His nervousness spiked when there was no answer. His hand slid down to the doorknob, opened it, and then stepped into the steam-filled room. The air was so thick inside that he could barely breathe. He spotted a switch for a built-in exhaust fan and flicked it on. At first glance, the frosted glass screen of the shower looked unoccupied. He lowered his gaze to discover the fuzzy shape of Lupe's tanned frame sitting on the tiled floor of the shower. Henry's chest ached with the need to protect and comfort his man. The thought came as unbidden. Henry had never once considered taking a life partner in all the years, and now wasn't the time to start. He opened the shower door and turned off the water simultaneously, pulling the towel from the rail. Henry held out his hand to encourage Lupe to stand, "Come on, Doc., you can't stay in here all night. Someone else might want some hot water too."

Lupe's hand firmly clasped Henry's, and a surge of energy raced through his system. His wolf growled inside Lupe's head, and not for the first time, 'Mine.' As the two men stood holding hands, neither one wanted to let go, even after Lupe was standing a few scant inches from Henry. His eyes leveled on Henry's full bottom lip, and he wondered what it would be like to kiss him. He licked his lips and held his breath. His mate's scent slid through his body like a slow-burning fire in his veins. He was aware that Henry hadn't made a move to step away from him either. Lupe needed something to take away his bad day. He needed to feel the comfort only his mate could give him. Acceptance.

CHAPTER 4

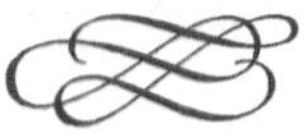

*H*enry fumbled with the towel, and it fell at Lupe's feet. As if caught under some strange kind of spell, his hand rose to cup Lupe's cheek. The sizzle of mutual attraction ramped up his desire to conquer, protect, and possess a part of someone, although he'd never wanted to own it before. That kind of connection with a person that made you crazy. His head lowered, and his teeth grazed Lupe's chin, "Tell me to stop, say you want me to leave, and I'll go."

Lupe shifted, aligning their naked chests. The intensity of skin on skin amplified his need to claim his mate, "Stay, I…."

Henry's lips covered Lupe's. They were strong yet soft. He was commanding and dominant yet gentle.

Lupe's first kiss took his breath away. With years of wants and needs, he responded with fantasies and daydreams. His tongue tangoed with Henry's while his hands slid cautiously around his mate's hips and down to the curve above his ass. Lupe sucked Henry's tongue as it probed his mouth. He tightened his hold pulling him closer. Lupe's naked backside hit the door as Henry spun them both quickly. Henry adjusted his pelvis so that Lupe could feel how much he wanted him, how much the younger man's beauty captured him. He broke their kiss to Lupe's bottom lip with a nip, making both men moan.

Henry rested his forehead against Lupe's and rolled his hips to get his attention, "Whatever you need Doc.," he nipped Lupe's earlobe. "An hour. A day. A week or a year Doc. I'll take whatever you're happy to give and I promise I'll give you what you need. If you'll let me." The words Henry had never said to another man tumbled freely from his lips as though he were begging.

Lupe's head spun, realizing that maybe the attraction between mates went way deeper than his brothers had let on. Everything seemed to be moving so fast, his mind and his heart traveling at the speed of thought, yet time appeared to be standing motionless. Should he have this overwhelming appetite to taste every inch of a man he'd only met a few hours ago? Lupe banished the fear associated with admitting he was gay. Placing all his faith in the mate bond, he spoke, "I want more, I want everything…" his face flushed and heated as he prepared his next words. "I've never…."

Henry's growled possessively, "You're killing me, Doc. I won't take you the first time against the bathroom door." He softly brushed his lips against Lupe's before taking a step back. Offering his hand, Henry led Lupe out of the bathroom and over to the bed. He turned to face the younger man. After grazing his teeth along Lupe's jaw and up to his ear, he whispered, "Do you trust me, Doc?"

Lupe moaned something incoherent, which Henry took as a 'Yes.'

"Lube?" Henry asked, and Lupe pointed to the bedside table, barely able to concentrate as Henry's teeth scraped his neck. His hardened shaft pulsed from the electricity that rippled through his body all the way to his soul. His heart pounded as he watched Henry flip the lid on the tube and squeeze a dollop onto the tips of two fingers on his right hand. Lupe's muscles clenched as lust ignited his skin, and his breathing became erratic with anticipation.

Henry licked his top lip, "I'm going to taste you now," Lupe snarled in appreciation of his lover's words. He sucked in his breath and held it as Henry's smooth tongue traced the crown of his throbbing manhood. Henry slid his left hand between Lupe's legs, cupping behind his right knee. He wordlessly instructed him to place his foot beside him on the bed. Henry's large hand curled around Lupe's thickness and lowered it away from his torso to enable him to swirl his tongue around it. He liberally covered it in his saliva before sliding it to the back of his throat.

Lupe gasped at the sensual sensation of being surrounded by warm velvet. He clenched his butt cheeks to regain control of himself so that he didn't cum and embarrass himself. Focusing on his breathing, he slowly relaxed. Henry sat perfectly still and allowed him to process the sensory overload. When Lupe's hips began to slowly glide himself in and out of Henry's mouth, he added a little suction and pressure to the tip with his tongue. Henry lifted his lubricated fingers to slide between his splayed ass cheeks. As he found the tight puckered ring, he smeared the slippery goo in circles, getting closer and closer to picking Lupe's flower. Lupe's hands rose to cushion Henry's head as he slid back and forth inside his mouth. He paused mid-stroke as the tip of one of Henry's fingers breached his darkest desire, working first one, then two of his slippery digits past the tight muscles at the entrance. He consolidated his thoughts in relaxing his body to allow the delightfully foreign intrusion.

Henry curled the tips of his fingers to stroke over that slightly swollen area on the forward wall of Lupe's passage, making

Lupe cry out in ecstasy. Henry growled in the back of his throat, making it vibrate around Lupe's harder than steel spike.

"Fuck! That… feels… too… Good." Lupe said with the need to cum growing closer but then still out of reach of the cliff. The added sensation of Henry's fingers teasing his prostate was driving him higher than he'd ever been before, yet his climax was so far, yet so close, all at the same time.

Henry took the lead, his head bobbing up and down on Lupe's shaft at the same time his fingers fucked his forbidden fruit. Gasping for air Lupe growled, he snarled as the heat tingled in his ass, and it surged from his balls along his shaft, exploding deep inside Henry's throat. His inner muscles contracted, and he cupped the back of his lover's head as Henry touched a part of him that had been cold and alone for far too long. Now he felt whole. He would always have this moment branded on his soul, mind, and heart. He felt claimed. His legs trembled, his hands shook, and he was light-headed. Henry released his satisfied cock and slid his fingers from his body. He curved his hand around Lupe's hip and licked from his navel to his nipple.

"I need to be inside you so badly I ache," Henry admitted.

Lupe moved onto all fours on the bed and presented his virginal asshole. Henry ran his shaky hands over the succulent globes before giving them a light squeeze.

"Not this time Doc, I want to see your face when I take you for the first time. Lay on your back for me."

Lupe sank down as instructed and watched as his mate climbed onto the bed and then up over his body to cage him in.

"If you say stop, I'll stop. Are you sure?"

Lupe skimmed his hands over Henry's ribs and down to his hips. Pulling the older man closer, "I need you." he whispered as he lifted his head to cover Henry's lips.

Henry broke the kiss and sat back on his haunches. Grabbing the tube of lube, he coated his throbbing shaft. He gently lifted Lupe's feet up to rest on his shoulders, then holding the bulbous tip of his cock at Lupe's entrance, he slid it around his partner's puckered ring.

A knock at the door made them both pause, holding their breath. A second knock followed only a couple of seconds later before the door cracked open halfway.

"Sorry dude, I didn't know if you had your headphones on. Umm sorry to interrupt, but there's someone at the front door to see you." Blaez stammered to make a quick exit.

CHAPTER 5

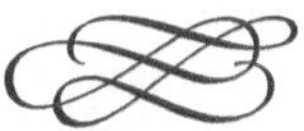

Blaez returned to where he'd left the man who'd introduced himself as Dr. Lucas James. Only the smug bastard wasn't there. He'd taken a seat on the couch in the lounge room. Blaez narrowed his eyes in distaste and leaned against the wall. Assessing the flowers in the man's hands, the fact he was there to see his brother, and the new evidence that had just come to light in Lupe's room. He had to assume that this smug bastard wanted a piece of what was going on in the privacy of his brother's bedroom.

"He'll be out in a minute," Blaez said, crossing his arms over his broad chest.

Lucas stood and gave him a cheesy smile, "Oh, that's fine, just point me in the right direction." he looked over Blaez's shoulder, then added, "I'm sure he won't mind."

"Well I beg to differ, sit tight." he growled.

Lucas's smile quickly melted away, and Blaez saw something in the man's eye that he'd seen a number of times. A sliver of concern for his brother raced down his spine, and he knew Lucas wasn't safe, and Lupe was this prick's target.

Blaez pulled his phone from his pocket and quickly sent a message to Lupe.

Dude,
   Bring your man with you!
   Blaez.

~

Lupe closed his eyes, "Fuck!"

"Your family didn't know." Henry stated rather than asked.

"No." He whispered, "They do now."

Lupe rolled sideways away from Henry, "Stay, I'll only be a minute. This…" he sighed and pointed between them, "Isn't finished."

He entered the bathroom to wash his hands, and after he'd rinsed his flushed face, he gripped the basin with both hands and bowed his head. His stomach flipped nervously as his phone beeped on the bench beside him. Henry's hands wrapped around his muscular frame as he stood and met his gaze in the mirror. One of Henry's hands settled over his heart and the other on his stomach. He felt safe in the older man's embrace, empowered even. He'd found the missing piece of his puzzle, and he didn't care what his brothers or anyone else thought, for that matter. He was keeping him.

He spun in Henry's grasp and claimed his lips with everything he had. Their tongues danced in a passionate promise of what was to come. Lupe broke the kiss to trail his lips along Henry's jaw. He briefly suckled his earlobe, then seductively moved down to the place where his muscled neck met his broad shoulder. The moment his mouth closed over his mate's dark skin, his wolf pushed forward, and his canines elongated. With a growl, he struck. He bit down swiftly, sucked once as he withdrew his bite, and then licked over his mark. "Mine."

When he leaned back to meet Henry's eyes, he found none of the confusion he felt. There was no judgment. He knew the look on Henry's face would lead them both into temptation. A place where Lupe would gladly follow if Henry were leading the way.

He also suspected that his brother would be back knocking on his door soon. He placed his hand on Henry's face, "I better go and see what the problem is."

Henry reluctantly released his hold, stepped back, and allowed Lupe to grab his phone on the way back into the bedroom.

Lupe unlocked his phone to find a number of missed calls and messages, two from the hospital's number. One from the Charge Nurse, a few from Doctor Lucas James and finally one from Blaez.

The only one he paid attention to was the one from his brother. He turned to look at Henry.

"What is it?" He asked.

"I'm not sure, but Blaez said to bring

you too." Lupe tossed his phone on the bed and removed two pairs of clean sweatpants from the drawer, tossing one to Henry and shoving his legs into the other pair.

Henry wasted no time in pulling on the soft cotton pants and stood waiting at the door protectively for Lupe. As he neared, Henry opened the door and then followed Lupe out of the room, with his hand reassuringly resting on his shoulder.

Lucas jumped to his feet as he saw Lupe. The shy smile on his face that didn't quite make it to his eyes slipped when he noticed Lupe wasn't alone. His demeanor shifted to sly rather than concerned or friendly. He held out the bunch of flowers for Lupe.

Blaez stepped between Lucas and Lupe and wrapped his hand around the floral bouquet, "I'll take those. They look a little limp." he said. "I'll put them in some water." as he turned his back on Lucas, he met Lupe's dumbfounded gaze. Blaez winked at his brother and smirked at his own jibe at the limp dick standing awkwardly in the lounge room.

"I... Um... I called in to see how you were doing... You know with the board's decision to do an autopsy and run an inquest into the death of such a high profile patient as the Senator. I'm sure it will be fine, I thought I could probably help, maybe go over your statement with you regarding your treatment."

"What?" Lupe frowned. This was the first he'd heard of it.

Henry stepped in front of Lupe, "My partner is a gentleman. I on the other hand am not. I strongly suggest you leave right now before I throw you out."

Blaez stormed back into the room, "No need, I've heard enough from this slimy little fucker." he grabbed the upper arm of Lucas' pressed suit and helped him find the door.

"Get your hands off me you thug... Lupe I can help you... Have dinner with me?"

Lupe stepped around Henry, "Blaez wait!" his brother paused momentarily. He frowned, his mind ticking over, processing the situation. "Doctor Lucas, are you saying that you can make all this simply go away if I have dinner with you?"

"It will be a start, yes." Lucas smiled and tugged at his jacket.

"Awesome," Lupe grinned. "Now if you could just do one thing for me before I kick you and your sexually inappropriate ass out."

"Wh… What?" Lucas stuttered.

Lupe lifted his hand and pointed above Lucas' head, "Smile motherfucker, and wave your career goodbye for the camera."

As Lucas stumbled out through the front door, he hit a wall of muscle. He staggered back and glanced up to almost swallow his own tongue. Tate's hand snapped out and grabbed the man's shirt to catch him before he fell. He snarled at him with dislike after hearing most of the conversation from outside. Then pulling him close, he growled in Lucas's ear, "Stay away from my brother."

Jasmine stepped out of the way as the man quickly escaped towards his two hundred thousand dollar car parked in the driveway.

CHAPTER 6

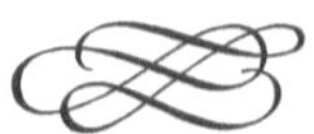

ate walked into the house with Jasmine. He looked from Lupe to Henry and raised an eyebrow. He almost cracked a smirk as both Henry and Lupe postured to protect one another against his wrath. Jasmine moved up beside him, and his arm automatically swept around her pulling her closer. He was about to speak as Houston burst through the front door.

"Who the fuck was that idiot? The son of a bitch almost ran us off the road as we drove in."

Lupe became emotional as his brothers began to converge in the lounge room.

"You knew," Henry directed his question

to Tate, who gave him a curt nod in response.

Lupe's eyes widened in shock. Tate glanced down at the woman standing at his side, then looking back at Lupe, he rolled his eyes, "You can't help being attracted to who you're attracted to." he winked.

Blaez chuckled, but secretly, he wished he could find that sort of connection with someone. His eyes flickered to the clock on the wall. Taking his exit, he said, "Later, I'm out of here. I have to get to work." he spun on his heel and made his way to the garage.

Houston looked at his partially dressed brother and then focused his attention on the Senator's bodyguard, Henry. His eyebrows lifted toward the ceiling as realization smacked him in the face. Cameron nudged him when she followed his sightline to find his gaze fixed upon a fresh mark, barely visible on the dark-skinned man's shoulder.

"You're staring," she whispered.

"Hmm," he turned to her, mildly distracted by his thoughts. "Sorry, what?" his attention quickly shifted to his mate's.

"You were staring," she repeated.

"Oh shit, oh no, no that wasn't what I was… processing." Houston tried to explain.

"Wow awkward much guys?" Lupe shook his head and glanced at Henry with a crushed expression on his face.

Tate was the first to move. He stormed across the room and gave both men a brisk slap on the upper arm, and then nodded. "Take care of him Henry, I'd hate to have to hurt you." Spinning on his heel, he cursed, "Hey does that mean…" his words instigated a look of fear on Lupe's face, giving his brother a growl. Tate narrowed his eyes as he guessed that none of that mate stuff had come up when Henry and Lupe had been to-gether. "Houston," he looked at the one who liked to think he had control over everything going on in the Five Brothers Security household. "What do you say you look into giving our currently unemployed friend here a job?"

"Sure, maybe tomorrow. I'm wrecked tonight." he said, stifling a yarn.

Jasmine silently walked across the room

and wrapped her arms around Henry, and lowered her head to rest on his chest. "I know you and my dad were close even though he was your boss, he was also your friend. We're going to miss him." she released her hold and wiped her eyes. Lupe shuffled his bare feet on the plush carpet, studying how the pile seemed to bounce back after being trodden on. Jasmine took a step to stand in front of Lupe, placing her hand on his cheek. She gave him a weak smile. "Don't feel bad Lupe, you did everything you could." she made a slight hiccup sound, and Tate was beside her instantly.

As her hand began to slide from Lupe's face, he captured it and placed a kiss to the butt of her palm, "Thank you." he said, meeting her sad eyes with his own, "If you need anything..." he trailed off suddenly, feeling as if nothing and no amount of knowledge could fix what had happened.

"Come on, Red, how about we get you home?" She allowed her mate to lead her to their vehicle. She didn't argue or fight when he lifted her gently into the passenger seat and put the seatbelt around her. The click not even reaching that fuzzy part of her brain that didn't usually do helpless well. Tate placed a tender kiss on her forehead before he closed the door and rounded to the driver's side. He drove them home to their new apartment in silence. When he parked and turned off the ignition, he asked, "Are you sure you don't want to go to a hotel?"

She shook her head. 'No.'

As they entered the living area where the Senator had earlier collapsed to the floor, Tate reorganized the furniture. Jasmine spotted the brown paper bag sitting on the lounge. At the sound of the bag unfolding, Tate turned to see what the noise was. His mate stood with tears running down her cheeks, staring at a blue rectangular box. He snarled, unhappy about whatever it was upsetting his mate.

"I think I'm gonna be sick," she dropped the items she'd been holding and ran for the bathroom. Tate snatched up the discarded things and quickly raced after her.

She was standing with her hands on her knees, leaning over the toilet.

Tate stood beside her, rubbing circles on her back, "Breath in… Breath out…" he continued to instruct her breathing, helping center her focus. After a few minutes, he stepped over to the basin and sat the stuff on the bench beside the sink. He ran a washer under the cold water and rang it out. He glanced at the blue box. 'Fuck!' It was a pregnancy test kit. He passed the wet cloth to Jasmine to wipe her face, and at the same time, he slid the offending packet into the third drawer. 'Maybe in a day or two,' he figured.

As Lupe closed the door to his bedroom, he sighed. "I wish we'd met under better circumstances."

Henry's hand cupped the back of Lupe's head as he pulled him closer. He rested his forehead against Lupe's, "I have to go. I have things that I need to take care of." his lips crashed down over Lupe's for a passionate minute. When he broke the kiss, he stripped out of the borrowed pants and tugged on his discarded suit with jerky movements. Lupe stood staring at the floor in confusion, but his pride wouldn't allow him to ask if and when his mate would be back.

He walked to the bathroom, and after he used the toilet, he returned to his room to find it empty, all bar the two quarter filled glasses of Glen. Lupe's chest ached as he poured one of the free poured nips into the other and then slugged it back, taking his breath away on a sob. "Fuck my life," he muttered and climbed into bed in hopes of waking up to find it had all been a bad dream.

Henry raced back to his hotel where he and the Senator were staying. The image of Lupe in bed tantalized his mind as he drove. His heart sped up. He couldn't explain the attraction for the younger man in words, it was just a feeling deep inside, and that was telling him he was the one. And if they were going to have a chance at something more than a fling, he had to take the matter of the Senator's death and Lupe's future into his own hands. Henry knew he couldn't leave things to be manipulated by a sleaze like Doctor Lucas James.

Inside his room, he collected the folder of important documents the Senator had made him carry with them in case of an emergency. After finding the particular reports and legal paperwork he was looking for, he fired up his laptop.

He called room service, ordered a light supper, and then worked. He hooked into the hotel's free Wi-Fi internet and began opening tab after tab. Each one with a different search criteria. An hour and a half later, he'd constructed all the evidence and reference material he could find, including the names of all the members on the board of the Bayside General Hospital and their financial backgrounds and skeletons also. He wished to speak to one, in particular, he was one of the boys, and he had a history with Doctor Lucas James.

Henry placed his empty tray outside the door while all the data he'd discovered was transferred onto a memory stick. He shut down the computer and put all the information and the documents he'd need for his meeting safely aside, ready to take with him in the morning.

He suddenly wished he'd taken the time to ask for Lupe's number. He would have liked to have heard his voice before going to bed. Even if it was only to check on him and see that he was alright, he stretched his body and felt a slight pull in the nook of his neck. His dick hardened at the thought of how passionate Lupe had been. It was as though a whole new world had been opened up to him, and he would experience the thrill of all the firsts like they were his own by taking Lupe as a new lover. The idea of being both in control of the taking and being taken made his body ache, and his skin broke out in a sweat. He entered the bathroom to prepare for a shower. He stood facing the mirror and had to admit that even at thirty-five, his body was fit, and his muscles were well defined. His dark skin was smooth, and he took pride in keeping it that way. He leaned forward to observe the mark on his shoulder, giving it a prod with his fingers. It was too hard with the color of his skin to see any bruising, but where Lupe's eyeteeth had broken the skin, there was an obvious mark. His cock twitched at the thought of his lover being so out of control that he'd bitten him.

Henry turned on the shower and stepped under the hot water. He closed his eyes and let the heat wash over his body. As he washed himself, his hand slid down to cup the weight of his seed bearers. He rolled them gently between his thumb and fingers. His other hand braced the tiled wall as he released his hold on his balls to circle his girth. His thumb and forefinger sitting underneath the crown of his circumcised shaft. He tightened his grasp and began to slowly pump his fist along his stalk, sliding the velvet skin over the cores sensitive inner nerves. He could see in his mind the man he wished was touching him, and he prayed it wouldn't be too long before they could be together. He desperately wanted to be Lupe's everything, first and last and always. Henry increased the pace of his strokes as he imagined Lupe's mouth and tongue licking his tip, then slowly working his cock between his lips to reach the back of his throat. His movements mimicking the magnificent scenes behind his closed eyes. The fantasy playing out in his head made his balls tighten, and he felt that knowing tingle of his approaching climax. As his rigid length throbbed and pulsed in his hand, he lowered his other hand down to apply pressure behind his testicles while continuing to cuff his cock. Delivering just the right amount of pressure to his perineum, he prolonged reaching orgasm. With the use of breathing techniques, in alliance with his vast experience in the art of self-satisfaction, he finally succumbed to the intensity of his postponed ebullience.

Henry felt the tension leave his body as his hot cum surged along his shaft and exploded from the head of his pulsating mast.

His breathing resumed its normal rate, and he finished his shower more determined than ever to take care of Lupe. He didn't just want to fuck him. He wanted to romance him. As he climbed into bed, he set his alarm to ensure he would be awake in time to secure his future. Then glanced at the empty side of the bed next to him. His hand brushed the untouched pillow, and he knew the bed beside him would not be empty for much longer.

CHAPTER 7

*H*enry sat with an elegant quietness outside the board-room for Mr. David Brookes. As the head of the hospital's board of directors, the man should have been above reproach. Therefore Henry could only assume that either Mr. Brookes was either still entangled with Doctor Lucas James or the doctor had some alternate means of controlling the situation. Nonetheless, Henry had no plans to leave before establishing his directive. Lupe was his, and he refused to allow a cocky prick like Lucas James, doctor or not, to get in the way of finding true happiness.

He'd never been one to believe in love

at first sight. Lust – Absolutely, but love? That shit was for fairy tales. He sighed with the resolve that whatever he felt for Lupe Garcia was more than a chemical reaction of hormones in his brain. He felt it all the way to the marrow in his bones. It was an inner glow, a calmness that washed over him at the thought of making his man smile. That is what his soul craved. With an equal amount of confidence and arrogance, he would do everything in his power to cock-block that sadistic motherfucker from ever getting his hands on what was his – Dr. Lupe Garcia.

Henry brushed the leg of his pants as the door to the boardroom opened, and the woman from behind the reception desk stepped out of the room.

"Mr Jackson, Director Brookes will see you now." she told him, holding the door open for him to enter.

"Thank you Dianne that will be all for now," Henry instructed, closing the door as he entered.

"Sir?" her voice could be heard through the closing gap as she wedged the toe of her stiletto in the rapidly shrinking space. Director Brookes stood from his seat in apprehension.

Before explaining, Henry glanced in his direction, "This is of a somewhat delicate nature." he lifted the leather case to demonstrate he hadn't come empty-handed. "Unless you'd like everyone in the hospital to hear about your connection to a young doctor Lucas James, I'd suggest that you call off your watchdog."

"It's fine Dianne. I wish to have a private conversation with Mr. Jackson. I will call for you if we need anything, you're dismissed."

"Oh, um, yes, sir." Dianne conceded, then removed her foot and allowed Henry to close and lock the door from the inside.

The Director resumed his seated position at the head of the table, clasped his hands in front of himself defensively, and then waited for Henry to begin.

As a tactical man, Henry decided against taking the seat at the other end of the table, which he knew would make the Director feel more comfortable. Instead, Henry walked confidently to the seat directly to the right of Mr. David Brookes and slowly slid the seat out from the table, and planted his ass right under the other man's nose. Taking his time, he sat the leather case on the table before slowly unlocking it with the combination.

"Now, I am not sure what your present arrangement with Dr. Lucas James is. However, I have evidence that explains a not so small incident that took place in another hospital prior to you being nominated to Bayside General Board of Directors. It would also seem that I have managed to find a paper trail which links you and Dr. James. Your decision to place him in charge of the cardiology department, even though the position was offered to a much more experienced college, was asinine. Who only looks to have stepped aside due to a nasty case of blackmail."

"And exactly what is your point?" David Brookes asked, taking a large swallow of a glass of water that sat on the table.

"It would appear that your naughty little doctor, has taken an unhealthy interest in someone close to me. I want that to stop, and I want it to stop now. Am I making myself clear? I have reason to believe that Dr.

Lucas James has reported Dr. Lupe Garcia for gross negligence in the diagnosis and treatment of my former employer, Senator Adam Winters. I have all the information here that is needed to clear Dr. Lupe Garcia of any wrongful doing, and in return I want to report Dr. Lucas James for sexual harassment within the workplace. I don't care how you do it, but I want it done by the end of business today. Find a hospital in Greenland for all I care, but after today he will no longer be a member of staff at Bayside General."

"But… But you can't do that. I love him. I have always loved him."

"Well more fool you, maybe you should get out more often. He is making an idiot out you and doing nothing to hide it. If you look inside the manila envelope, you will see what he really thinks of you. I found those pictures plastered all over the internet and the moron thought it was cool to photo bomb some of the images. Get rid of him before he ruins whatever's left of your reputation along with his own. Just make it all go away and fast."

Henry slid a second envelope over with

a copy of the Senator's personal physician's report and a copy of his medical directive that stated, 'Do Not Resuscitate.'

"Dr Lupe Garcia did nothing wrong, I want the investigation halted immediately, and the case shredded. There is to be no permanent record against his name, except to say that he was propositioned by Dr Lucas James in front of me, immediately after the Senator's death. You will find that both of the documents I have provided you with, are also signed by the Senator and witnessed not only by myself, but also the Senator's long-time friend and High Court Judge Joseph Langdon." Henry stood from his seat, "That concludes my - You show me yours and I'll show you mine. As you can probably tell, Dr. Lupe Garcia means a lot to me and I will do everything in my power to ensure his safety. Now if you would be so kind as to excuse us, I do believe that Dr. Garcia is taking a personal day and I have a lunch date. Thank you for your time."

Director David Brookes had begun to look somewhat pale throughout the conversation. He fidgeted with the call button on the phone sitting to his right on the desk, finally pressing the one that would link him to the receptionist outside.

"Dianne, please page Dr. Lucas James to my office immediately and send a message to Dr. Garcia to notify him that his personal time has been approved and we will see him bright and early on Monday. Thank you."

Henry sat behind the wheel and suddenly cursed himself. He had the contact number for Tate. He quickly sent a message to him asking for Lupe's number. His phone beeped within minutes of him hitting send. Tate had simply forwarded the details from his contact list, asking no questions. Henry saved the information into his contacts list and placed it in his favorites. Then hit the call button, and he left a brief message when it went straight to message bank.

Lupe had switched his phone off after taking the call from Director David Brookes. He'd been stood down pending an investigation. He wished he'd gotten Henry's number before leaving the night before. He rolled out of bed, then stood stock still staring at it.

He'd come so close to claiming his mate, but that was yesterday, and today his man was nowhere to be seen. He tossed a towel over his shoulder and headed to the gym, thinking that maybe a run would help clear his head. An hour later, he still felt lost as to what to do. How was he going to deal with the situation of his mate? He'd bitten Henry, which meant he'd claimed the man as his life partner, his mate. But that didn't mean Henry would ever make a counterclaim. He wondered what it meant if Henry did. Would he then take on the curse the same way his brother's women had? Would Henry become a werewolf…? Even for a man of science, a doctor, he had no fucking idea.

In the end, Lupe decided to shower and change, then head into the city to the hotel where the Senator and Henry were staying at.

Henry stopped at a gas station on the way to Lupe's. He'd never dated before, so he had no idea what to get for someone who fit the category of Mr. Right. After circling the shelves twice, he decided on a bunch of flowers and a box of chocolates. Wasn't that what most men got for their dates?

He arrived at the Five Brothers headquarters to find Houston out the front washing his truck. "Is Lupe home?" he asked.

"Yeah, he was just headed to his room when I came outside. Just cut through the garage and let yourself in." he smiled.

Henry jumped out of his SUV and collected the things he'd brought with him. He locked up his vehicle and gingerly made his way to where he knew Lupe's room was located. When he knocked on the door, there was no answer. He opened it just far enough to make out the sound of water coming from the bathroom. He let himself in and stashed his bag in the bottom of Lupe's walk-in robe, unsure of how much time he had left before Lupe would be out of the shower. He quickly made the bed and placed the box of chocolates in the center of the pillows and the flowers on the bedside table. Unsure what kind of reception he would get, Henry, kicked his shoes off next to the side of the bed that he hoped like crazy he would call his own, then hid in the walk-in robe and waited.

~

Lupe walked out with only a towel wrapped around his hips to find a beautiful bunch of flowers beside his bed and a box of chocolates on his pillows. He picked up his phone and switched it back on. He unlocked the screen when he saw he'd missed a call from an unidentified number. With his hand shaking, he hit redial, and as he lifted the phone to his ear, he heard music coming from his closet. "What the fuck? Henry, is that you?"

Henry walked out of the closet with his phone in his hand. "Yeah, it's me. I wasn't sure how to go about any of this, so I'm just going to wing it. Okay?"

"Sure, I'm listening." Lupe put both hands on his hips and waited.

"I was wondering if you were free for lunch, I know of a great restaurant not far from here, I thought we could talk and get to know each other better." Henry offered.

"How about we cut to the chase? I know what I want, how about you...." Lupe's words were cut off as Henry rushed at him, his lips crashing down over Lupe's. As Lupe opened his mouth in a surprised gasp, Henry slid his tongue inside to dance passionately with Lupe's. They both moaned; Lupe's hands rose to tango with Henry's clothing as his fingers grew busy unbuttoning buttons and opening zippers. Within minutes Lupe had Henry naked, and Henry was returning all of Lupe's passion.

CHAPTER 8

*D*octor Lucas James paced back and forth in the boardroom. He ran his hand through his hair with frustration.

"You can't do this to me! It's just not fair. Who does this guy think he is?"

"It would seem that he is the one holding all the aces up his sleeve. My hands are tied. I suggest you take the deal I'm offering you, pack your bags and get your passport ready. It will make things easier for us all in the long run." Director David Brookes instructed. After careful deliberation and considering all the information Mr. Henry Jackson had given him, he had no alternative than to cut the young doctor loose. The deal he'd offered him was as sweet a deal as it would get for either of them, especially if they were going to come out of this with their reputations intact.

David had called an old friend in England and had taken him up on the offer of an exchange program that Doctor Simon Calmity had put forward to the board at Dunn Place Hospital. The program was designed to exchange skills and knowledge by swapping doctors between Australia and England to broaden their training and techniques.

Doctor Lucas James was the first doctor to be sent abroad from Bayside General. It would effectively eliminate all the present issues he had created. Even though David Brookes was going to miss his good time boy, he'd taken what Mr. Jackson had said, processed it, and realized that he could do much better than a manipulative playboy.

Henry rested his head against Lupe's and whispered. "Doc, I want it all, the house, the white picket fence, everything. But I only want those things with you. I know none of this is making any sense, and I probably sound as though I'm babbling, but...." Lupe silenced his mate by moving his thumb from Henry's jawline up to cover his lips.

"It's okay, I feel the same. But... before we go any further we need to talk. I can't take your right to choose away from you, we need to have everything out in the open, if we are going to make things solid between us."

"Then maybe we need to get out of here, because I won't be able to think straight as long as we are both naked, not when I want you so bad it hurts." Henry admitted.

"Lunch it is then," Lupe smiled, cupping Henry's cheek, and brushing his lips against his mates. He lowered his eyes to see Henry's thickened shaft pulse with desire. With a sigh, he stepped back and then spun on his heel to grab something to wear for their date.

Henry walked into the closet and retrieved a pair of jeans and a casual button-down shirt, and a comfortable pair of shoes.

Lupe looked only slightly stunned as Henry began to dress in front of him. Within a short while, they were ready to leave. When Lupe opened the door to exit, Henry wrapped his arm around Lupe's waist pulling his back flat to his chest. He nipped Lupe's neck and then flicked his earlobe with his tongue.

"I'll drive Doc, we still need to pick up your ride from Tate's."

Lupe could feel Henry's desire against the center seam at the back of his jeans, making the teeth of his zipper bite into his hardened shaft just a fraction more. They both moaned, and Lupe rested his head backward onto Henry's shoulder. "We could always stay here, you know?"

"Not if we are going to talk first, and I'm hoping you will ask me to stay the night, there will be plenty of time to make good on the demands of our bodies."

The waiter escorted them to a table on the deck overlooking the water. "Will this do, sir?"

Both Henry and Lupe said in unison, "Yes. Thank you."

Henry pulled out Lupe's seat and waited for him to sit down, pushing his chair in under him as a gentleman should. He then took his own seat opposite him.

"Can I get you gentlemen something to drink?" the waiter with the name tag saying Thomas asked.

"I'll have an iced tea. Thanks, Thomas," Henry said while driving.

"Make that two thanks," Lupe added after a quick glance at the list of beverages.

Thomas moved to offer a menu to Lupe, and as he opened his mouth to speak, Henry politely cut him off. "Thanks, Thomas, but I'd like to order for the both of us."

Lupe relaxed against the back of his chair. As the corner of his mouth lifted in a smirk, he crossed his arms over his broad chest, and his eyebrow rose with curiosity.

"We'd like the Oysters Kilpatrick for entrée, followed by the rib eye fillet reef and beef, while I believe dessert will be served at home," Henry said in an official-like manner.

With the pleasantries of ordering their meals out of the way and the service of their drinks sitting on the table near them, Lupe could not have been more at peace yet more on edge at the same time than he was at that moment. He was trying to put the words in order of importance in his mind. He'd always been a little on the systematic side of chaos.

They both took a sip of their drinks and then tried to speak simultaneously, "I...."

"I... Sorry you go first." Henry offered.

"Oh um, okay. I'm not sure how to explain what I need to tell you, and you will more than likely think I'm absolutely certifiably insane by the time I'm finished. But try to keep in mind I have irrefutable evidence back at the house, it might just help preserve what you think of me right now, in this moment."

Lupe explained his drive to become a doctor and how he'd lost his mother. The way he'd met his brothers and how they were all connected by their common father, Venom Black. He eased into the background of the curse his family carried and described his affliction and its link to the moon's cycle. Lupe made a mental note to never play poker with his mate as Henry's facial expressions never altered once during the entire conversation.

"The conundrum that I face is obvious, yet also elusive. The embarrassing predicament is that," he paused, then cleared his throat to continue with a blush. His eyes focused on the area he knew he'd bitten Henry, currently covered by his mate's shirt. "You see," he lifted his hand to tap his own shoulder as an indication. "I have already asserted my claim on you. The instant my teeth broke your skin, I sealed my own fate. It is part of the curse that once I have initiated taking a mate, I cannot change my mind. My future happiness now balances on whether or not you will accept or reject my claim. If you choose to accept, then you should be aware, that things could go either way. I am only surmising, but there is a strong possibility that you will be infected by the curse, in the same manner, that my brother's mates have been."

Henry sat back in his chair with a massive sigh. It was the first time throughout the one-sided conversation that he'd made so much as a sound.

"This pull that I can feel towards you,

the need to be near you. It began the moment I opened the door for you at Jasmine's. Just to be clear, what happens if I walk away?"

Lupe studied the remnants of his main course before speaking, his meal now sitting heavy in his stomach, although it had been delicious. His chest also became burdened by the weight of Henry's question, making it hard for him to breathe.

"I'd only be guessing, but from what I've heard, I won't be able to get hard for anyone else." Lupe folded his napkin from his lap, "Ever." he sat the napkin on his plate, finished the remaining sip of his iced tea, which consisted of the melted ice in the bottom of his glass, then stood. "Thanks for lunch. It's been, for want of a better word… Interesting." He pulled his wallet from his back pocket and flipped it open to pay for their food.

Henry quietly stood and moved next to Lupe. He gently touched Lupe's wrist. "Please, Doc, don't run. That's not what I was saying."

Lupe met Henry's gaze head-on with a

confused look across his brow, "Okay, so what were you saying?"

"I'm… This is all new to me, I've never done the relationship thing, as I've previously told you. I wanted to know if you could walk away from me, if I commit to you, this, us. I won't tolerate another man touching you once you're mine. You're mine. Now let's get out of here so I can make that happen."

Lupe released the breath he'd been holding and was about to mention stopping in at Tate and Jasmine's to collect his vehicle. The thought was quickly chased from his mind as Henry lifted his hand and placed a kiss on his open palm.

"We'll get your ride tomorrow Doc." He then nipped Lupe's thumb, leading him toward the exit after passing a couple of large folded bills to the waiter, saying, "Keep the change."

CHAPTER 9

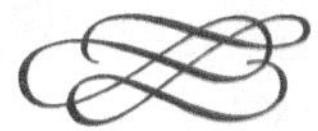

From the split second, the door to Lupe's bedroom was closed and locked, Henry was removing items of clothing and stalking his man. He'd popped the top button of his own jeans, and his hand scrunched the collar of Lupe's button-down shirt backing him against the closed door. Henry's lips covered Lupe's as Henry tried to show Lupe all the things he hadn't been able to put into words, using his action to speak for him instead.

Clasping the fabric firmly in his grip, Henry split Lupe's shirt straight down the center. Buttons ricocheted around the room, bouncing off of the furniture and fittings. Their lips never separated for a single moment as they lost themselves in each other's feel, touch, and taste.

Lupe wrestled with the fly on Henry's jeans, carefully lowering it so as not to pinch the swollen bulk of manhood beneath it. As Lupe slipped his hand inside Henry's underwear to cup his smoothly shaved balls, Henry's hand closed around Lupe's wrist. He broke their kiss with a moan, "I want to be inside you so badly," he gasped as Lupe softly rolled his jewels with his fingers. "I'm about to come in my jeans."

Lupe raised an eyebrow in disbelief that he had had that kind of effect on someone. The moment Henry slid his hand down the front of Lupe's pants, he realized they were equally turned on by the other. They would be perfect together, and all of his inhibitions and fears were shoved into a little black box in the back of his mind, where he locked them up and tossed away the key. Henry was his mate, and no matter what happened, at least he would have this memory of their time together if Henry should choose to walk away.

"Take it all off," Lupe instructed, nipping Henry's neck as his back bowed and he thrust his pelvis forward, pumping his shaft through Henry's firm grip.

Both of them admired each other's physique as they removed their disheveled clothing. Lupe threw his phone into the drawer beside the bed after switching it off, with no intention of being interrupted this time. He collected the tube of lube from his drawer and set it on the bedside table within easy reach. He then leaned back onto his bed and spread his legs in a comfortable position with one knee bent and curled his finger at his man.

"Come closer, I won't bite." he smiled. "Unless you want me to."

"Maybe, but I definitely do." Henry responded with a smirk as he placed his knee on the foot of the bed and prowled slowly towards Lupe.

Lupe's heart sped up as Henry trailed his tongue from the base of Lupe's throbbing ruler to the tip of its crown. He lolly-popped the bulbous head three times before sliding Lupe's cock to the back of his throat. He moaned, knowing the vibrations would create an irresistible sensation for his lover. Then with a deliberate calmness to his manipulations, he allowed Lupe's polished cylinder to escape his pursed lips to rest against his abdomen.

Henry caged Lupe's frame to reach for the lubricant, watching as his velvet-covered steel sword brushed against Lupe's satin-covered saber.

"God, you're beautiful," Henry exclaimed, sitting back on his haunches between Lupe's spread thighs. He locked eyes with Lupe as he covered his shaft with the slippery goo, ready to claim his man. Then with astute attention to detail, he prepared Lupe's virginal ring, teasing his rim with his slippery lubricious fingers until Lupe's fists were scrunching the bedsheets and his hips were wriggling to get closer.

"More… Please… I… I need you," Lupe breathed heavily with a burning desire that had become a raging fire within his blood. He wanted to be claimed, and he wanted it now. A growl rose from deep within his chest as Henry slid first one finger inside his tight ring and then another. Working them slowly in and out. There was a slight burn as his hole was stretched, it felt good, but it still wasn't enough. He needed more. Words eluded him, and he didn't know how to explain to his mate what he was feeling or what he wanted.

Henry sensed it was time. He leaned over and kissed Lupe gently, "Relax, Doc, close your eyes and just feel." he instructed as he slid his fingers free and aligned the head of his eagerly awaiting shaft. Holding his length securely, he applied just enough pressure to breach the ring of muscle at Lupe's entrance. Lupe moaned from the foreign sensation. His hands lifted from where they had been scrunching the bedsheets to cup behind his knees, presenting himself to his lover. Henry perched on his spread knees, then threaded his forearms under Lupe's legs, "I got you, Doc, just let go. I want to see you touch yourself while I make you mine."

Lupe released his hold, lowering one hand to rest on Henry's knee, holding him securely at the right angle. His other he curled around his pulsing manhood. Henry slowly rocked his hips until he was balls deep inside his man. Waiting perfectly still while his man adjusted to the pressure, the sensation of being filled by a lover. When Lupe began to slowly pump his shaft with his growing need to cum, Henry mirrored his motions.

"Fuck! You feel so good, Doc. I… I…" his words broke off as Lupe cried out in orgasmic ecstasy, and his sphincter contracted rhythmically around Henry's shaft, taking him over the edge along with Lupe. His hot seed pulsing inside the man he wanted to spend the rest of his life with, curse or no curse. Still connected, Henry lowered himself over Lupe and kissed him passionately.

"You're mine Doc, now and forever," he stated. As the last of his seed surged free of his shaft, Henry sank his teeth into Lupe's left pec, right over his heart.

At that moment, for the first time in his life, Lupe felt as though he belonged. He finally understood his brother's bonds with their mates. He fell asleep in the arms of the man he would spend the rest of his life with, his lover and his mate. Knowing that when the time came to test the curse, they would still be side by side, man to man or wolf to wolf.

75

###

ABOUT THE AUTHOR

Melissa Bell *lives in Brisbane, Australia. She has loved to read since the age of twelve when she discovered 'To Kill A Mocking Bird', previous to reading this book she hated reading. With a couple of handfuls of years and thousands of books later she wanted to try writing.*

She has most recently accomplished making the USA Today Best Sellers List in October 2021. And has now set her sights on reaching the NY Times Best Sellers List.

She enjoys good food and good company when she's not trying to concentrate on what she's writing. She loves to laugh as laughter makes the world go round not money. Unfortunately laughter doesn't pay the bills unless you're a really well-known stand-up comedian. Which she is not. She is hoping that this is the start of an exciting adventure as a published Author, and that maybe something amazing will come of it. She would like to invite you all to join her on her journey.

ALSO BY MELISSA BELL

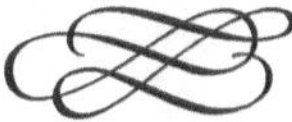

Please keep an eye out for other books by
Melissa Bell.

DUTIFUL GODS SERIES

Book #1 Destiny's Fate

Book#2 Taming Destruction

Book#3 Morpheus's Dream

Book#4 Defying Death

Book #5 Cosmo's Universe (TBA)

FIVE BROTHERS SERIES

Book#1 Houston

Book#2 Felan

Book#3 Tate

Book #4 Channon

Book #4.5 Lupe

Book #5 London

Books still to come in this series include – Blaez and Brody amongst others. (So stay tuned)

OTHER TITLES

Demon Hunters Series

Book #1 Shane